When Anna Leonowens makes the journey
to Siam with her young son Louis, she little
knows what life holds in store. It is 1862, and the
King of Siam is a modern monarch who wants
her to teach his children Western ways and ideas.
His cruel Prime Minister, the Kralahome, has
different views, because **his** power rests on the
dark forces of magic, superstition and fear.
He also wants to be king himself.

Published by Ladybird Books Ltd
27 Wrights Lane London W8 5TZ
A Penguin Company
3 5 7 9 10 8 6 4 2

LADYBIRD and the device of a Ladybird are trademarks of Ladybird Books Ltd

TM & © 1999 Morgan Creek International Inc.

Printed in Italy

Ladybird

In 1862, the journey by sea to Siam took a long time. But Anna and her young son Louis soon began to enjoy their voyage. Louis even made friends with the ship's monkey when he saved him from drowning. Then suddenly, a terrible storm blew up.

Siam's evil prime minister, the Kralahome, made it worse. From his sorcerer's den in Bangkok, he conjured up a terrifying sea serpent from the clouds to frighten the new schoolteacher. But Anna wasn't in the least afraid — and neither was Louis!

The storm blew itself out, and soon Anna and Louis were in Bangkok. The Kralahome and his assistant, Master Little, came to welcome them in the royal barge. When Louis said goodbye sadly to Moonshee, the ship's captain told him he could keep the monkey. Louis was delighted. So was Moonshee!

Anna and her son were taken straight to the palace. "You'll be shown to your quarters," said the Kralahome.

"But I was promised a house of my own, outside the palace," objected Anna. "I must remind the king. I will take nothing less than I was promised."

"You will tell king this?" asked the Kralahome, surprised.

"I will tell king this," said Anna firmly.

As Anna and Louis were going into the throne room, the Kralahome stopped them with upheld hand. "Burma sends a gift to the King of Siam," he said.

In front of the king was a Burmese nobleman, with a beautiful young girl beside him. "A *gift*? That *girl*?" asked Anna, outraged at the idea.

Then the king saw Anna. "Who? Who? Who?" he asked.

"I am Anna Leonowens, the teacher you sent for," said Anna.

"Yes, yes," said the king. "Come!"

He proudly showed Anna round the great palace, pointing out a printing press – a laboratory – a train – and even a hot air balloon.

Although Anna was impressed, she did not forget her own problem and she said, "I want the house I was promised, your Majesty."

"You teach in palace, you shall live in palace!" And the king stormed out.

Anna was furious. She went to her room and found some of the king's servants unpacking her cases. "Please don't unpack," said Anna. "I'm *not* staying."

She wandered over to the window to look out at the beautiful gardens. In the distance she could see the Burmese girl and a young man. Even from a distance, she could tell they liked each other.

Standing beside Anna, the king's first wife shook her head in disapproval. "That's Tuptim, the new servant girl. Servant girl and crown prince is forbidden. Against tradition!"

"Long ago, every tradition started as something new," said Anna. She smiled as she looked at the young couple. Anna wished them well.

That afternoon Anna went into the throne room to tell the king she was leaving. Everyone was gathered there.

"The children come for presentment," said the king.

Anna began, "But your Majesty, I'm not staying…"

"Silence!" growled the king, and Anna had no choice. She stood quietly beside the king as the children came forward one by one. They bowed to the king, then touched Anna's hands to their foreheads. Each one was so gentle and sweet that Anna's heart melted.

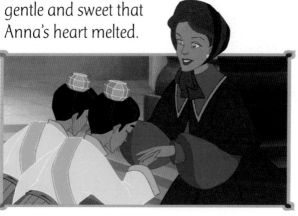

At last they all bowed to her and the king, and Anna sighed and took off her bonnet.

The king said, pleased, "Our school teacher has changed her mind. She will live in the palace."

"But only for the time being, your Majesty," said Anna firmly.

The moment the Kralahome heard that Anna was going to stay, he seized his chance to make trouble. He wrote to tell the British envoy, Sir Edward Ramsay, that the new teacher was in danger from the barbaric King of Siam.

He was sure the British would come and the king would fight them. The Kralahome might be king yet!

Meanwhile, Anna had taken the royal children to see the wonders outside the palace for the very first time. They made friends everywhere they went in the city.

But the king was furious. He told Anna he didn't like the way she was teaching his children — and no, she couldn't have her own house!

Anna was very upset and decided to go back to England.

When the crown prince went into the throne room, the king was still angry.

"Father," said the prince, "how can Siam be modern if you keep to old ways?"

"Old ways?" spluttered the king. "What? What?"

"Well," the prince went on, thinking of Tuptim, "would you for example, like in the old dark days, choose a wife for your son?"

"Of course!" said the king. "As my father did."

Then he took off the royal pendant that he wore and gave it to his son.

The prince was surprised. "But father… is for king to wear."

"Now future king will wear!" said the king.

"As future king, I believe I should have right to choose wife."

"Impossible," replied his father, and the prince went away.

In the garden, Louis was chasing Moonshee. When he heard sounds of kickboxing, he peered over a bush and saw the prince practising with one of the guards. When the guard went away, Louis came forward. "Let me try!" he said.

"No, no, you'll get hurt," laughed the prince. But Louis kept trying, and suddenly he punched the prince on the nose. The prince was shocked.

"Oops!" said Louis. "Just a lucky punch!" And he went away to find Moonshee.

As the prince bent down to a pool to wash off the blood, Tuptim came up. "You are hurt!" she said. Then she saw the royal pendant. "Oh, you are crown prince! You, me, is forbidden." But the prince took off the pendant and hung it round her neck, as a token of his love.

Not far away, Master Little watched with interest. Then he went to tell the Kralahome.

While Anna was packing, the prince came to see her. He asked her to go to his father, who had had bad news. Although Anna was still furious, she went to the throne room. "Has there been any news recently?" she asked.

"News? Yes!" said the king. "The British call me a barbarian."

"It's a lie!" said Anna. "What have you decided to do about it?"

"Guess!" said the king.

Anna said carefully, "I believe — you won't do battle with the British. I think you are going to invite them to a ball so that you can prove how civilised you are."

"That's just what I had decided! They will see scientific experiment as well," he added proudly. "Air travel!" He looked at Anna. "You will arrange," he ordered.

Then — at long last — Anna was promised her own house, outside the palace.

The idea of a ball upset the Kralahome's evil plan, but he soon formed a new one. In the meantime, Anna went to work with a will. She even showed the king how to dance.

When the great evening arrived, everything went smoothly to start with. But as soon as the Kralahome mentioned the royal pendant, the king told his son to show it to the British envoy, Sir Edward Ramsay. And of course the prince no longer had it!

Then the Kralahome told the guards to bring in Tuptim.

She was wearing the pendant, and the king was so furious that he wanted to whip her. But he threw the whip to the floor, and the prince and Tuptim ran for the door. Louis helped them to escape, and followed them.

The Kralahome ordered the guards to go after the three to make sure they never returned! The prime minister knew that the British would lay the blame for their deaths at the king's door.

Tuptim, Louis and the prince – not forgetting
Moonshee – ran for their lives. First they
went over the rooftops, and then through
the jungle on the elephants. But the
Kralahome and his guards were in control,
although the runaways didn't know it. They
were herded towards the river – and soon
they were in it, heading for the rapids.

But the king had decided to take a hand. He
flew by in his hot air balloon, and soon
rescued them.

Sir Edward Ramsay was watching through a telescope, and hailed the king as a hero.

Just at that moment, the Kralahome hit the balloon with a firework, and down it crashed. Although the others were safe, at first everyone thought the king was dead, and started to cry. Then he opened his eyes and said, "I will say when is time to cry."

Later that evening, Anna went to see the king. He was in bed, surrounded by his children. He spoke to the crown prince. "Chululonghorn, rise! Now, suppose you are king. What would you do?"

"First, I believe that learning is a good thing for everyone. Secondly, no more bowing like toad before king. And…"

"More?" asked the king.

"All persons shall have freedom to marry who they want. Even a royal prince!"

Tuptim came in, and took the prince's hand.

"Some day you will be great king," smiled his father.

But one person was no longer in line to be king—the Kralahome, because everyone knew how wicked he had been. He had been put to work in the elephant stables—and the elephants didn't like him!

～～

At last Anna got her new home— outside the palace. "I'm speechless!" she said when she saw it. "For once!" said the king. He went on, "At banquet, we did not dance. Now, shall we dance?"

And so Anna danced—and danced— and danced, with the King of Siam.